To Bob, Sammy, Ben, Louie, and Heather
With Love
In loving memory of my brother Gregory Beall, one of my biggest fans.

Dear Friends,
   This book was created as a result of my experiences as a neonatal intensive care nurse. It was written during my schooling to become a family nurse practitioner as I worked towards my Master of nursing degree.
   I hope that this story will be useful to both yourself and your children, patients, colleagues and friends. The feelings discussed in this book are significant for children of all ages, including adults. Even young children may use the pictures in the book to create their own stories.
   Please use this book as a tool to allow others to express their feelings and most certainly to explore your own.
   Thank-you for sharing this story with others-

Published by: Bopar Books, Park City, Utah
www.himynameisjack.com
Text and illustrations © 2000, 2005, 2010 Christina Beall-Sullivan and it's licensors.

ISBN 0-9759718-0-8
This book is written to provide information that the healthy siblings of a chronically ill, disabled or dying child may experience. This book should not be used as an alternative to receiving professional advice and assistance.

Hi, my name is Jack and I am eight years old. I have a mommy, a daddy, and a little sister named Molly. Molly is five and has been sick many times since she was born. Molly has an illness that makes her sick quite often.

This means that Molly has to go to the doctor more than other kids. Sometimes Molly is so sick that she has to go to the hospital.

Having a sister that is sick is sometimes hard for me.
I bet it is hard for you sometimes, if
you have a brother or a sister or a friend who is sick.

My mommy and daddy have to spend a lot of time with Molly especially when she is very sick. This makes me feel lonely sometimes.

When I feel lonely I can draw pictures for Molly and my mommy and daddy. Molly can have pictures in the hospital. It is O.K. to feel lonely sometimes.

When Molly is sick everyone gives her presents and lots of attention. This can make me feel very jealous.
(I wish I was getting all of those presents!)

It makes me feel better to help Molly open her presents. I even help her play with them.
It is O.K. to feel jealous sometimes.

I feel angry when my mommy and daddy are too busy to play with me because Molly is sick. Sometimes I feel angry when I have to do extra chores because Molly is sick.

When I feel angry I ask my mommy and daddy to talk with me. Sometimes we can look on the calendar and write down a special time that will be just for me.

During this special time maybe we will go for a walk, or go fishing, or cook a yummy meal. It is just nice to be together.
It is O.K. to feel angry sometimes.

Some days Molly is more sick than others. When she is really sick and has to go to the doctor or to the hospital, I get really worried and scared.

I worry that Molly is sad.
I worry that my mom and dad are sad.
Sometimes I even worry that Molly will
never come home.

When I worry it makes me feel better to talk to my mom,
or dad or Molly. Even talking to them on the phone
can make me worry less.
It is O.K. to worry sometimes.

Sometimes when I feel angry or jealous or lonely or worried, I get really mad at Molly for being sick. I may even be mean to Molly when I am mad that she is sick.

After I am mad I often feel guilty. I feel guilty because I know it is not Molly's fault that she is sick. I feel guilty that maybe I make Molly more sick when I am mean to her.

My mom tells me "Jack, it is not your fault that Molly is sick. You are never the reason Molly gets sick. Everybody gets mad sometimes, but this does not make your brother or sister sick." I feel better after I talk to my mom or dad.

I have a lot of different feelings about my sister being sick. All of my feelings are normal. Many boys and girls have a brother or a sister that is sick like Molly. Many boys and girls have the same feelings as me.

When I feel lonely, jealous, angry, worried or guilty
the best thing I can do is tell my mom or dad.
Then we can take some time and talk about my
feelings.
This always makes me feel better.

No matter how I feel sometimes, I know that
my mommy, daddy and Molly love me all of the time,
and I love them back.

The author received her Bachelor of Science degree in Psychology from Mary Washington College in Virginia in 1991. Her Bachelor of Science in nursing was obtained from the University of South Carolina in 1996 and she completed her Master of Nursing degree at the University of Utah in May of 2000. Currently she, her husband Bob, daughter Sam, infamous basset hound Bogart, and portly pug Parley reside in Park City, Utah.

For ordering information please go to:
www.himynameisjack.com or
email the author at christina_beall@yahoo.com

ISBN 0-9759718-0-8